P9-BJY-299

RECEIVED
NO LONGER PROPERTY OF
JUN 28 2022
SEATTLE PUBLIC LIBRARY
IDC LIBRARY

To Meme and Papaw (Barbara and Haskell),
who knew the way home.
John 14:6

DIAL BOOKS FOR YOUNG READERS • An imprint of Penguin Random House LLC, New York

First published in the United States of America by Dial Books for Young Readers,
an imprint of Penguin Random House LLC, 2022 • Copyright © 2022 by Hannah E. Harrison
Dial and colophon are registered trademarks of Penguin Random House LLC.
Visit us online at penguinrandomhouse.com

Penguin supports copyright. Copyright fuels creativity, encourages diverse voices,
promotes free speech, and creates a vibrant culture. Thank you for buying an authorized edition
of this book and for complying with copyright laws by not reproducing, scanning, or distributing
any part of it in any form without permission. You are supporting writers and allowing Penguin
to continue to publish books for every reader.

Library of Congress Cataloging-in-Publication Data is available.

ISBN 9780593324172 | Manufactured in China • 10 9 8 7 6 5 4 3 2 1

TOPL

Designed by Jason Henry • Text set in Aptifer Sans • The artwork for this book was created with
Winsor & Newton Designers Gouache on toned tan and gray Strathmore 400 Series 184 lb. mixed
media paper with vellum surface.

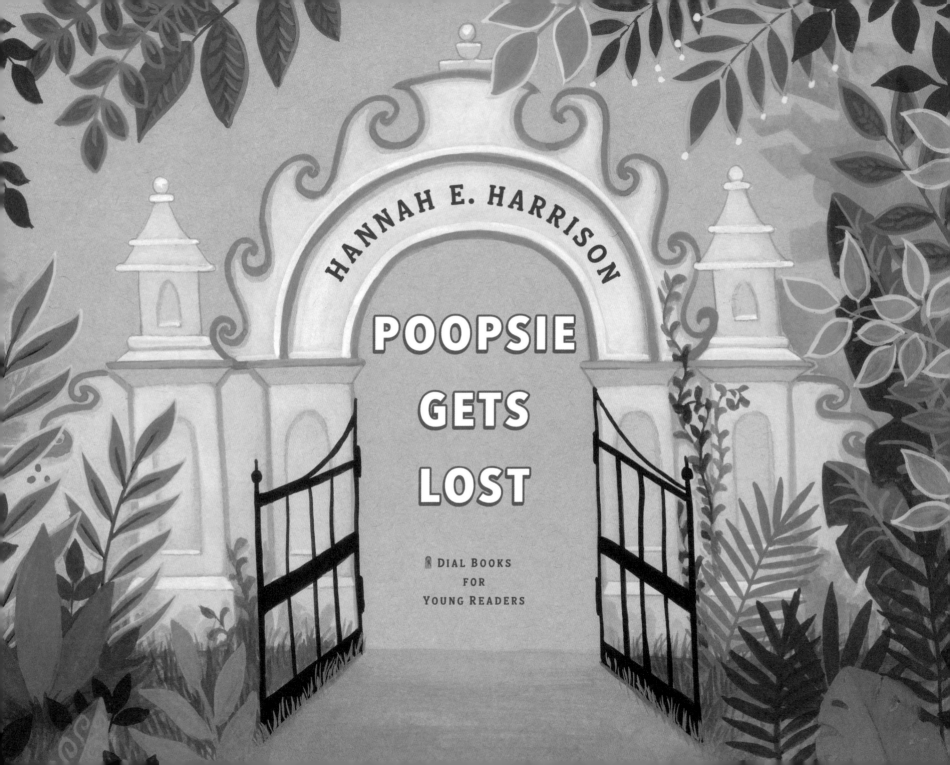

HANNAH E. HARRISON

POOPSIE GETS LOST

DIAL BOOKS
FOR
YOUNG READERS

Poopsie the cat
sat on her cat bed.

She licked her paw.

She rubbed her ear.

She licked her paw again.

She made a weird gurgling noise.

She licked her...oh, Poopsie.
This is sooo boring!

Don't you want to do more than just
sleep, and eat, and look fluffy all day?
There is a whole world out there!

Tell me, Poopsie—are you a *snoozy* house
cat or are you a *daring adventurer*?

That's what I thought.

See that flap in the door over there?

This may surprise you,
but it's called a cat door.

All you have to do is push it,
and out you'll go!

That's it...

You did it! Good for you!

Smell that, Poopsie? That is the sweet, sweet, smell of freedom ... mixed with a little bit of doggie-doo.

Now, I know your humans probably told you
never to leave the yard, but that's only because
they are party poopers.

Fortunately for you, I know where the *best* fun is.

Wait—you don't know how to read, do you?

No?

ENTER AT
OWN RISK

DANGER

UNMARKED
TRAILS

Good. Keep going.

I say, it is rather creepy in here.
I hope you don't get eaten by anything...

Oh, *never* mind—you'll be fine. Excitement is just to the right.

Oh, Poopsie, look—a lovely vine hanging from a tree!

You should swing from it— like a wild thing!

Well, I have to say, that is the *best* impersonation of a vine I have *ever* seen.

Also, are you all right, Poopsie? You're looking a bit bushy.

Ah! A slightly pungent and
murky river—how picturesque!

Simply hippity-hop across from rock to rock.
Go on—it'll be like hopscotch!

Egad! Those rocks have eyes and teeth! Talk about masters of disguise—those rapscallions even fooled *me*, and *I'm* smart!

Aww, look—a clump of sleeping pussycats! You should boop one of them on the nose. Don't be shy—how else will they know you want to be BFFs?

Nope!
They are *not* fans of the boop!

Run, Poopsie, RUUUUUN—like your nine lives depend on it, because they really do!!!!

Quick—into that mysterious cave!

Out of the cave!

Through those delightful bushes!

Over that quaint-looking bridge . . .

Oops.

Well, Poopsie, this is a fine pickle
you've gotten yourself into.

I know you wanted adventure,
but this is all a bit much,
don't you think?

Oh, don't be such a sourpuss.
Look at all the fun we're having...

Poopsie . . .

You're not going to go *home*, are you?

. . . what are you doing?

I hope you're not allergic to pollen.

Are you trying to look like a tiger
or a circus peanut?

I'm guessing this is the part where you get eaten, never to be seen again.

You should probably turn around.

So, apparently you wrestle crocodiles now?

**Fine! Go home if you want to—that's where all the fuddy-duddies are!
You should fit right in!**

Poopsie, if you go back through that gate, I will never speak to you again!

Oh, well, congratulations—you've made it
back to snooze-ville.

Don't let the cat door hit you on your backside.

I suppose you're going to want to celebrate with a thrilling nap.

... Actually a nap doesn't sound that bad. It was exhausting watching you almost get poisoned, and eaten by crocodiles, and mauled to death by tigers, and...

...Poopsie, I hope you are not thinking about closing this book...

Poopsie, I wouldn't do that if I were...

...well that was rude.